PETIT PURR FINDS A HOME

Written by Violet Trouern-Trend
Illustrated by Kevin MacDonald

Dedicated to Malek and Christy

Story © 1996 by Violet Trouern-Trend
Illustration © 1996 by Kevin MacDonald

Published by Puddleboots Publishing
ISBN 1-888145-00-5
Library of Congress Catalog Card Number 96-071707
Printed in Korea

Puddleboots Publishing, P.O. Box 193, Weatogue, CT 06089
(860) 651-0069

When Mary Goodpicture arrived at her studio to open up and finish painting her beautiful portrait, she was surprised to find huddled on the doorstep, four small fluffy kittens.

She wanted to pick them up but decided to wait for their mother to return, who she was sure had not gone far.

Mary Goodpicture finished her beautiful portrait and left her studio for the day. To her great surprise, the four small fluffy kittens were still where she had seen them earlier in the day.

"I can't leave you here", she said to the kittens lovingly.
"There's a big storm coming and you're already cold and hungry,
I bet. I can not keep you for long; but don't worry little ones. I'll
find a home for each of you."

At that moment she pulled her big green woolen cap off her head, picked up the kittens and placed them all carefully together in the big cozy cap.

She then started walking towards Rainbow Park, where she knew many children and their parents came to play at the end of the day. She would especially like to see a family she had often talked with when she went there to feed the ducks or to get an idea for her next painting.

And much to her pleasure they were there.

"Good Afternoon, Mrs. Bellefleur," said Mary Goodpicture, "I was hoping to meet you here."

"Good Afternoon, Katherine and Michael."

And she told them how she had found the four little kittens who were trying to climb out of her big woolen cap as she was speaking. "I am wondering if you can help me find homes for these adorable kittens."

And very soon she was surrounded by children, all wanting to see the kittens.

"Oh, please let me hold the little gray one", said Katherine.

Mary Goodpicture lifted him out of her cap and placed him in Katherine's arms. She held him close.

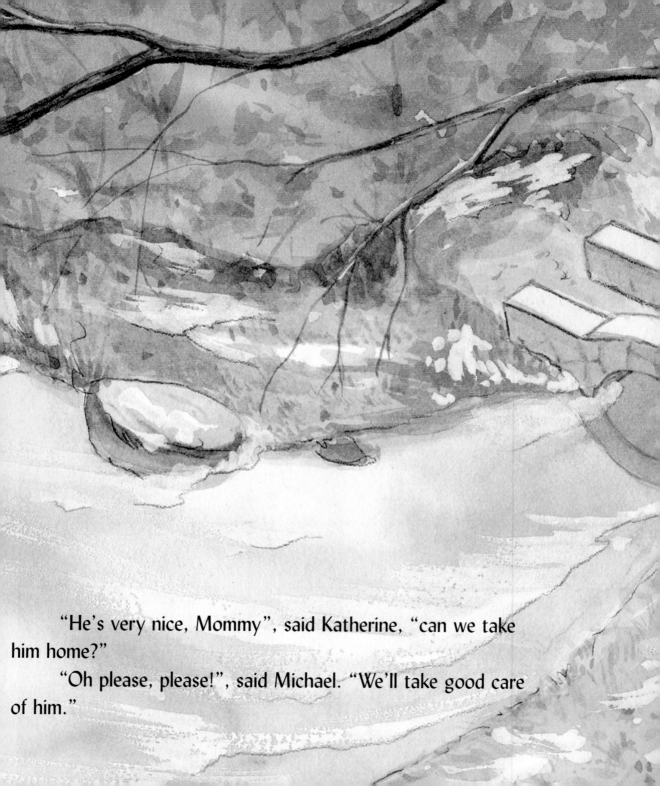

"He's very nice, Mommy", said Katherine, "can we take him home?"

"Oh please, please!", said Michael. "We'll take good care of him."

Mrs. Bellefleur smiled, looking at each of them fondly.
Then, she looked at Mary Goodpicture and said, "OK, we will
take him home. I hope you find homes for the other three."

"We'll call him Petit Purr", said Katherine. And Michael
agreed.

Before long, Mary Goodpicture had found three families who took the other three kittens. She folded up her green woolen cap, put it in her pocket, and walked home thinking that maybe she would paint a park scene with many children, playing and skating on the pond…

..and, perhaps a lady with a green woolen cap full of adorable kittens.

THE END